Hamish
Hides Out

Also in this series:

Hamish Hides Out

Linda Jennings
illustrated by Kate Aldous

MAGI PUBLICATIONS

for Lesley
LJ

for Evie
KA

First published in Great Britain 2002 by
LITTLE TIGER PRESS
1 The Coda Centre,
189 Munster Road, London SW6 6AW
www.littletigerpress.com

Text © Little Tiger Press, 2002
Illustrations © Kate Aldous, 2002

Kate Aldous has asserted her right to be identified as
the illustrator of this work under the Copyright,
Designs and Patents Act, 1988.

A CIP catalogue record for this book
is available from the British Library

Printed and bound in Great Britain
by Bookmarque Ltd.
Set in 16.8pt Goudy

1 3 5 7 9 10 8 6 4 2

Contents

Chapter One

Hamish loved his home. His cage was set on a table in the living-room, so that he could see everything that was going on around him. He had a wooden house, where he slept during the day, and an exercise wheel, where he played at night. It was Hamish's favourite time. He enjoyed his busy exercise on the wheel, and when he had finished, he would sit on his back legs and look out into the moonlit

garden and the strange, green space that the family called 'lawn'.

The family came into the room during the day, to have their meals and watch television. The little human called Alice was his favourite. She brought him food and filled his bowl with fresh water. Sometimes she took him out and let him run up her arm or round the floor, exploring. She would watch him carefully. There were so many places in the room where Hamish could get lost, or be caught by his old enemy, the big black cat, Boris. Ever since Alice had caught Boris licking his lips and staring up at the little hamster, the door was kept closed. But Boris sometimes sneaked into the living-room when no one was looking. Once he jumped on to the table and stared through the cage bars at Hamish.

"Yum, yum, supper," he said, trying to push a clawed paw through the cage bars.

Hamish jumped back, out of reach.

"You'll have to be cleverer than that," he said, sticking out his tongue. "The bars are far too narrow for you to catch me."

One night, when the family had gone to bed, Hamish was busy doing his frantic exercise on the wheel.

Suddenly THUMP! Boris jumped on to the table, skidding towards the cage.

CRASH! The cage wobbled on the edge of the table and then toppled to the ground. Poor Hamish clung to his wheel as everything turned upside down. His cage lay on its side, the lock broken and the door open.

"At last!" purred Boris, stretching out a sharp claw.

Hamish let go of the wheel and fled for his life. He scrabbled out of the cage and skidded across the room. Boris followed.

Hamish scampered here and there, wondering where he could hide. Though he knew the room well, he did not know where he could be safe from the hungry cat. He dived under an armchair.

It was a good move. Though Boris tried to hook him out, he couldn't reach the hamster.

"I'll find a way to get you!" hissed Boris. "Don't think you'll be safe anywhere."

Hamish crept further under the chair. He managed to pull on a bit of loose lining and climb right inside the chair. He crouched there, trembling. When would it be safe to return to his cage?

Then he remembered. The cage lay on its side, on the floor, with the door open. What could he do?

Chapter Two

Hamish curled up inside the chair and tried to sleep, but it was no good. He was very hungry, and it was a long time till morning. Perhaps he could get to his food bowl? He quietly wriggled from the lining of the chair, dropped to the ground and looked across the floor. Boris had gone, but he remembered now that he had eaten his supper before he'd gone on his exercise wheel. Alice always brought his food into the living-room from somewhere else. Perhaps he could find out where.

Hamish crept very cautiously across the room and out through the partly opened door. He stopped for a moment, woffling his nose. Could he smell cat? No, but he could smell human food!

Hamish made his way quickly down the dark corridor and into a strange room. Something was going on in there. There were rustlings and the sound of feet pitter-pattering across the floor. At least it didn't sound like a cat. Then Hamish saw an animal, rather like himself, scurrying to and fro, gathering up scraps of food.

"Who are you?" he asked.

The animal stood on his hind paws

and wrapped his long tail round himself.

"I could ask you that," he said. "You're not a mouse like me. And you don't live here in the kitchen either."

"I'm a hamster," said Hamish. "The cat knocked over my cage and it's not safe to go back."

"Cage?" cried the mouse. "You live in a cage? How awful!"

"It's nice and safe – or was," replied Hamish. "And Alice brings me food." He gave a pathetic squeak. "I'm *terribly* hungry."

"Well, there's plenty of food here if you look for it," said the mouse. "Cheese, a few grapes, some nuts. Those humans are very messy. They don't like us coming into the kitchen and taking the food, but we keep well hidden. If you help me find some more, then you can share it with me and my family. We all live under the floorboards. I've got fourteen brothers and sisters."

Fourteen! Hamish was horrified. For as long as he could remember he'd lived alone. He *liked* living alone. He couldn't

imagine what it would be like with so many others around him.

"My name's Percy," said the mouse, who was already piling the scraps into a heap. "Come on. Let's try the rubbish bin next."

Hamish and Percy managed to squeeze their way under the sink and open the lid of the bin.

"Ugh!" said Hamish, wrinkling his nose.

"Delicious!" said Percy, pulling out some potato peelings. "Look, take that apple core. It's gone a bit brown, but it will taste OK."

Hamish was used to his food coming from a packet. The apple core had some loops of long slimy stuff twined round it. It looked horrible, but he took the stalk and pulled it to the floor.

"Well, that's enough," said Percy. "Take what you can carry and I'll get some of my family to bring back the rest."

Hamish nibbled at a slice of cheese. Hm, not bad. Ignoring the disgusting-looking apple core, he took the slice in his mouth and followed Percy across the floor to where he could see a small hole in the floorboard. Hamish and Percy squeezed through it and into a dark, dusty, scary-looking passageway. Something with lots of spindly legs scuttled across their path.

"Help!" cried Hamish, nearly dropping the cheese. "What was that?"

"Only a spider," said Percy, hurrying on. "It won't hurt you."

Suddenly the passage opened out into a large space. Sixteen pairs of bright, beady eyes stared out at them.

"Hello, everyone," said Percy. "Here's the first of the goodies. Some of you can go back and bring the rest."

Hamish was still holding his piece of cheese when one of the mice rudely snatched it from him.

"I don't know who you are," she said, "but we share everything here. No cadging the best bits."

"Don't be so mean, Ginny," snapped Percy. "This is my friend, Hamish. He's been helping me gather together food for you all."

Although Ginny had talked about sharing, she wouldn't let go of the piece of cheese. "There's plenty more out there," she said.

"Well, go and fetch it then," said Percy. "Hamish has worked hard to find your supper. This is his reward."

"She never helps," said Percy's brother, Max. "She's just selfish."

"I do, so there!" snapped Ginny. "And to prove it, I'll do as you say." She flounced off after the others.

Hamish heard them chattering and quarrelling as they went. He wondered again how Percy could bear to live with so many brothers and sisters.

Chapter Three

"Help yourself," said Percy's mum
when the mice had returned with
more food. "Just choose what you like.
I don't expect you're used to mouse
food."

Hamish looked at the other mice
nervously. Would they all protest as
Ginny had? But, to his surprise, they sat
back politely as he helped himself to
another, larger piece of cheese and a
juicy grape.

Ginny had run into a corner with the apple core.

"She's welcome to it," thought Hamish.

Next morning, Percy and Max showed Hamish round the many little holes and passages that led from their home. They both scampered ahead of him, chattering excitedly.

"Don't leave me behind," called Hamish. "I'll get lost."

"Hang on to my tail," offered Max. "That's what I did to Mum when I was tiny."

The mice never stopped talking and squeaking as they showed him more passages and more holes into other parts of the house.

"That's the hall," said Max. "We

don't go there much. No food."

"And this is the living-room," added Percy.

"That's where I live!" cried Hamish in excitement. He squeezed in beside the two mice and peered out through the mouse-hole into the room. He saw the chair where he had hidden from the cat. He saw the television and the table.

But where was his cage?

Perhaps the family thought Hamish was never coming back again. Or, more likely, they had probably taken it away to be mended.

"What shall I do?" he wailed. "I've got no home now."

"You can stay with us," said Percy. "That would be great!"

Hamish liked the two mice and their mum and dad, but he still wasn't sure he would like living with such a large and noisy family.

"That's kind of you," said Hamish. "But I think I'll hide in the chair till Alice comes back."

"It's not safe," warned Max. "Not with that cat around."

"He's not often in here," said Hamish.

"Alice knows he wants to catch me, so she keeps the door closed. Unless she forgets, of course. But I think I'll risk it."

The room looked very quiet and peaceful in the morning sunshine.

Before the mice could say anything else, Hamish darted across the floor.

"Goodbye," he called to them. "Thanks for everything."

The morning wore on and Alice didn't appear. Hamish was beginning to feel hungry again. He heard the door slam and guessed the family had gone out.

"I'll go back to the kitchen," he thought. "There may be some more scraps around." Hamish scampered across the floor towards the door.

He was only halfway across the room when he met Boris!

"Help!" he squeaked, then froze with fright.

"Ah, there you are," said Boris softly. "The family thinks I've eaten you. Well, now's my chance!"

He opened his big, pink mouth and lashed out with his claws.

This time, the little hamster was in far greater danger than he had been in his cage. His feet unfroze. He dodged past the black cat and, by luck, found himself beside the mouse-hole.

Boris was quick, but not quick enough. When his large, heavy paw came crashing down, Hamish was already inside the hole. Boris only succeeded in catching the very tip of his tail.

Chapter Four

In the darkness beneath the floorboards Hamish felt completely lost. He had been led through so many passages by Percy and Max; he now had no idea of how to find his way back to the mice again.

He licked his sore tail and wondered what to do next. He longed for the sound of Alice's voice. He longed for his water bowl, his food and his exercise wheel.

Sadly, he pattered down the dark passage to see if there was a safe way back.

Hamish found something at last. There was a missing brick in the side of the passage and a beam of sunlight flooded in.

He poked his head through the hole.

"The garden!" he cried. He didn't know whether to be excited or

frightened. It seemed so huge, with the green stretch of lawn ahead of him. Should he risk it?

"Well, it's better than being lost in those creepy passages," he said, as he squeezed out into the fresh air.

He was on the lawn, that great green space he had seen through the window. The damp, tickly grass felt strange under his feet. The birds, whom he had often watched from his cage, were swooping and crying overhead.

"I hope that they don't attack me," thought Hamish, but they were flying down to a birdbath. Some splashed in the water, some perched on the edge and drank. One hung from a tree, pecking a bag of nuts.

Hamish looked up longingly. He liked

nuts and he was by now dreadfully hungry. "You couldn't spare me some of those, could you?" he asked.

The bluetit looked down.

"What sort of animal are you?" it wanted to know. "You're not a mouse or a squirrel."

Hamish explained about the cat and the cage and being lost beneath the floorboards.

"Huh! I thought a cat might be behind it. It's not a big, black one with green eyes, is it?"

"Yes," said Hamish. "That's Boris. He's tried often enough to catch me, but he nearly got me this time."

"He'd eat us, given half the chance. But we're too quick for him."

Hamish wished he could climb up the

birdbath and have a drink, but his paws scrabbled and slid on the smooth stone.

"I'll send some water down, if you like," said a blackbird, helpfully.

Hamish opened his thirsty mouth and SPLASH! the blackbird flicked big drops of water into it. One hit Hamish in the eye, but he was grateful for the bird's kindness.

The bluetit dropped him down some nuts.

The birds were so busy helping Hamish that they didn't spot the danger until it was too late.

Boris poked his head out from the bushes. He wiggled his bottom, then sprang.

CRASH! He landed on the edge of the birdbath. The blackbird, taken by surprise, was trapped under Boris's heavy paw.

"Help!" she cried, as she flapped helplessly under the cat's paw.

Boris seized the blackbird in his jaws and leaped down to the ground. He didn't see Hamish sitting there.

"Ow!" he howled, as the little hamster nipped him painfully on the leg.

As Boris opened his mouth the blackbird fluttered weakly to the lowest branch of the tree.

"Be careful! It's not safe there!" warned the bluetit. "Cats can climb trees easily."

But Boris had forgotten all about the blackbird. He'd seen who had bitten him. "You again!" he snarled. "Well, a blackbird would make a nice tasty morsel, but it's you I'd like the best. You won't get away from me this time!"

Hamish was unable to move. There was nowhere to run to.

All around him, the birds were shrieking and fluttering.

"Save him!" cried the blackbird.

The commotion had attracted many more birds to the scene. Blackbirds, sparrows, starlings, bluetits and pigeons flew through the air in a big, angry cloud, and swooped down.

The birds pecked at Boris and beat him in the eyes with their wings. They landed on his back and dug in their claws.

Boris shook them off and fled over the fence into the next garden.

But the chase wasn't over yet. The birds and Hamish looked on to see a terrified black cat scrambling up a high tree with the neighbour's dog barking at the foot of it.

"Serves him right!" cried the birds.

"Thank you for saving my life," gasped Hamish.

"And thank you for saving mine," called the blackbird, as she flew off, high into the blue sky.

Chapter Five

"Now what?" Hamish wondered. It wasn't safe in the house and it wasn't safe in the garden. Perhaps he should try to find his friends, Max and Percy again. But the dark, dusty passages under the floorboards frightened him. He felt he could be lost in them for ever.

Hamish walked across the lawn. The gates at the end of the driveway were open and beyond them Hamish could see humans walking past.

Suddenly, something large and red swung into the drive and roared towards him. It was too late to get out of its way. Hamish could only crouch there, shivering with fear as the monster approached. There was a nasty smell and a loud, throbbing noise. Oil dripped down on to his soft fur. The

monster didn't harm him, though. It passed over him and travelled on towards the house.

Hamish was still too frightened to move. Was there nowhere he could be safe and quiet? The red monster had stopped now. Some humans climbed out of it, slamming doors. One of them was Alice – and she was carrying his cage!

Hamish gave a squeak of delight and scuttled towards her. But before he was even halfway there Alice had gone inside the house with the family and closed the door.

"So they're home again," thought Hamish. "Now all I have to do is to get back inside."

Hamish had had so many adventures

since yesterday, and had walked further than he had ever done in his whole life. By the time he reached the house he was so tired that he curled up beside a drainpipe and fell asleep.

When Hamish awoke, it was getting dark.

He peered up into the black mouth of the drainpipe. "I wonder if there's a way in here? It must lead somewhere."

He decided to try it.

The inside of the pipe was slippery and steep. Hamish scrabbled and scrambled and had just made a bit of progress when he was hit by a great rush of water.

"Oh, I'm drowning!" he gasped, as the flood swept him off his feet and back to where he had started.

He was soaked to the skin, but somehow managed to crawl away from the pipe. "Well, that's no good," he sighed. "There's nothing for it but to go back through the hole in the wall."

Very tired now, Hamish plodded round the house till he came to the missing brick. "I may be lost for ever in here," he sighed. "But at least I'm safe from Boris and from red monsters and floods of water."

He squeezed inside.

Chapter Six

Hamish peered down the passage. If he walked for long enough, surely he would come across one of the mouse family again. He wondered if he should call out to the mice and whether they would hear him if he did.

He was just plucking up the courage to do so when he heard the light pitter-patter of feet.

A mouse!

Hamish's heart lifted as it came

rds him. "Max?" he asked. "Percy?"

o, stupid, it's Ginny. Can't you tell the difference between us?" She looked him up and down. "You're in a bit of a state," she said. "Your fur is all greasy and wet. Where have you been?"

"Everywhere," said Hamish. "Under the floorboards, in the garden, up a pipe –"

"There's no need to boast about it," said Ginny. "You're stupid to get into such a mess. Well, do you want to come back with me or what?"

"What I really would like . . ." began Hamish, but thought better of it. Ginny was a difficult little mouse. If he said he wanted to go home, she might abandon him and disappear.

"Yes please," he said humbly. He

followed Ginny along the passage, trying to keep up with her fast, pattering feet.

At last they were there.

Ginny's mum gave a cry of surprise when she saw the wet little hamster following along behind Ginny.

"Hamish!" she cried. "You're back. Percy was really worried about you and that cat."

"Where is Percy?"

"Out looking for supper," said Father Mouse. "All the young mice have gone – except for Little Miss Madam here, who thinks herself too grand to look for food. Anyway, they'll all be back with plenty, so you must share supper with us again."

As he spoke, a familiar chattering

noise could be heard along the corridor.

"Save that raisin for me. That's my favourite."

"Right, swop the raisin for a bit of cream cracker."

Percy, Max and the others came into sight, laden with food. They were delighted to see Hamish again.

"Have you come back to live with us? Or are you still looking for your cage?"

"My cage has been mended," said Hamish. "But I don't know how to find my way back to it."

"We'll show you," said Max. "But have some supper first."

"Not the cheese – I want the cheese."

"Shut up, Ginny. Hamish is our guest and must have first choice. Help yourself, Hamish."

"I'd rather like to get back home right now, if you don't mind," said Hamish.

"OK," said Percy. "We'll show you."

Chapter Seven

Hamish was so tired that he could hardly keep up with the two mice. He clung on to Percy's tail, hoping he would soon be home. At last they reached the hole in the floorboard.

"Here you are then!" said Max cheerfully. "Safe and sound."

"Are you *sure* he's safe?" asked Percy. "Is that cat around?"

"No, the door is tightly shut – and the cage is back on the table," said Max.

Hamish knew he could never get back into the cage on his own, because the door would be locked.

"I'll hide under the chair," he told his two friends. "Then, when Alice comes into the room, I'll scamper up to her."

"Would you like us to wait here until she comes?" asked Percy anxiously.

Hamish felt a warm glow. How good it was to have friends who really cared about him. He had never known that feeling before.

"I'll be all right," he told them. "Don't worry about me."

He wondered if he would ever see Max and Percy again. Once he was back in the cage, he would never be able to visit them. He did, though, think of some way in which he could repay them.

"Come back tomorrow night," he told them. "I can push some hamster food through the bars to you."

"That's a good idea. We can keep in touch then. I bet hamster food's delicious," said Max.

Hamish said goodbye to his friends.

He was so pleased they wanted to visit him.

"Thanks for everything," he said, as he scampered under the chair.

From here, he could only see the top of the cage. But he could hear a noise. Creak, creak, creak, it went.

"That sounds like my wheel," thought Hamish. "But how can it be if I'm not in the cage?" It was a big mystery. Hamish glanced towards the door. It was firmly shut. Then he climbed up the chair, so that he was level with the cage.

Hamish could hardly believe his eyes.

There was another hamster inside the cage. It was going round and round on his exercise wheel!

Chapter Eight

The hamster stopped exercising. It looked out happily at the moonlit garden, as Hamish had done before. Then it turned round and saw Hamish perched on the arm of the chair.

"Hello," it said cheerfully. "What are you doing out there?"

"I'm wondering what *you* are doing in my cage," replied Hamish. "How did you get there?"

"My cage," said the hamster. "My owner bought me yesterday."

Hamish couldn't believe his ears. Had Alice replaced him already?

"My name's Harry," the hamster went on. "What's yours?"

"Hamish," he said grumpily, and then scuttled back down underneath the chair to sulk.

Hamish had liked living alone. He didn't want to share his cage with anyone. He felt hurt and angry. *Why* had Alice bought a new hamster?

Then he remembered something Boris had said. "The family thinks Boris has eaten me!" he squeaked. Perhaps that was why.

At that moment the door opened and Alice walked in, carrying some hamster food.

"Here she is!" Harry called down to Hamish. "Come and have breakfast!"

Hamish thought about the large, friendly mouse family. He thought of how warm he had felt when Max and

Percy had shown how much they cared about him.

Harry sounded as friendly as Max and Percy. But how would he feel about sharing his cage with a strange hamster?

Perhaps he should give it a try.

Very slowly, Hamish crawled from underneath the chair.

"It's me!" he squeaked to Alice. "I'm home again!"

"Hamish!" she cried. "I thought you were dead!"

Hamish felt her warm, caring hands scoop him up and take him towards the cage, he felt a wet tear plop on to his fur.

"Mum! Dad!" Alice called. "Hamish is back!"

"There's plenty of breakfast for both of us!" Harry told him, touching his nose through the bars. "Plenty of room in the cage, too!"

Alice smiled and opened the door, and Hamish scuttled inside.

It wouldn't be easy to live with another hamster. It wouldn't be easy to share his cage and his exercise wheel. But Hamish thought of Ginny. What a selfish little mouse she was! He wouldn't like to be like that.

"I'm sure everything will be fine," he said in a small voice.

The two hamsters were busy cleaning their whiskers after their meal when Harry sat up straight.

"Who's that?" he squeaked.

Hamish looked. Pressed up against the outside of the window was a black nose.

"*Two* of you!" Boris hissed. He scratched his claws on the glass, but of course he couldn't get in.

"That's my old enemy, Boris," said Hamish.

"Look him in the eye," said Harry. "Cats hate being stared at."

Both hamsters glared hard at the black cat without blinking.

Harry was right. Boris turned away and began to wash himself furiously.

"YAH BOO!" cried Hamish and Harry, dancing in their cage. "SILLY OLD BORIS!"

Boris slunk off into the bushes.

"Hurray! I don't think he can manage two hamsters at once," said Hamish, laughing. "Let's go inside our house, and I'll tell you all about my adventures!"

For more information about books
from **Little Tiger Press** or for our
catalogue please contact:

Little Tiger Press
1 The Coda Centre
189 Munster Road
London SW6 6AW

Tel: 020 7385 6333
Fax: 020 7385 7333
E-mail: info@littletiger.co.uk

Or visit our website:
www.littletigerpress.com